PENGUIN BOOKS

THE GREEN MILE: PART 2
THE MOUSE ON THE MILE

Stephen King, one of the world's bestselling writers, was born in Portland, Maine, in 1947, and was educated at the University of Maine at Orono. He shot to fame with the publication of his first novel, *Carrie*, and his subsequent titles include *The Shining* and *Misery*, which have all been made into highly successful films. He lives with his wife, the novelist Tabitha King, and their three children in Bangor, Maine.

Watch out for Stephen King's *Rose Madder*, out soon in paperback from New English Library, and his new novel *Desperation*, coming shortly in hardback from Hodder & Stoughton.

The Mouse on the Mile is the second in a novel of six parts. The first volume, *The Two Dead Girls*, is also published in Penguin.

STEPHEN KING

The Green Mile

PART TWO

The Mouse
on the Mile

PENGUIN BOOKS

PENGUIN BOOKS

Published by the Penguin Group
Penguin Books Ltd, 27 Wrights Lane, London W8 5TZ, England
Penguin Books USA Inc., 375 Hudson Street, New York, New York 10014, USA
Penguin Books Australia Ltd, Ringwood, Victoria, Australia
Penguin Books Canada Ltd, 10 Alcorn Avenue, Toronto, Ontario, Canada M4V 3B2
Penguin Books (NZ) Ltd, 182–190 Wairau Road, Auckland 10, New Zealand

Penguin Books Ltd, Registered Offices: Harmondsworth, Middlesex, England

Published simultaneously in the USA in Signet and
in Great Britain in Penguin Books 1996
1 3 5 7 9 10 8 6 4 2

Printed in England by Clays Ltd, St Ives plc

1

The nursing home where I am crossing my last bunch of t's and dotting my last mess of i's is called Georgia Pines. It's about sixty miles from Atlanta and about two hundred light-years from life as most people—people under the age of eighty, let's say—live it. You who are reading this want to be careful that there isn't a place like it waiting in your future. It's not a cruel place, not for the most part; there's cable TV, the food's good (although there's damned little a man can chew), but in its way, it's as much of a killing bottle as E Block at Cold Mountain ever was.

There's even a fellow here who reminds me a little of Percy Wetmore, who got his job on the Green Mile because he was related to the governor of the state. I doubt if this fellow is related to anyone important, even though he acts that way. Brad Dolan, his name is. He's always combing his hair, like Percy was, and he's always got something to read stuffed into his back pocket. With Percy it was magazines like *Argosy* and *Men's Adventure*; with Brad it's these little paperbacks called *Gross Jokes* and *Sick Jokes*. He's always asking people why the Frenchman crossed the road or how many Polacks it takes to screw in a lightbulb or how many pallbearers there are at a Harlem funeral. Like Percy, Brad is a dimwit who thinks nothing is funny unless it's mean.

Something Brad said the other day struck me as actually smart, but I don't give him a lot of credit for it; even a stopped clock is right twice a day, the proverb has it. "You're just lucky you don't have that Alzheimer's disease, Paulie," was what he said. I hate him calling me that, Paulie, but he goes on doing it, anyway; I've given up asking him to quit. There are other sayings—not quite proverbs—that apply to Brad Dolan: "You can lead a horse to water but you can't make him drink" is one; "You can dress him up but you can't take him out" is another. In his thickheadedness he is also like Percy.

When he made his comment about Alzheimer's, he was mopping the floor of the solarium, where I had been going over the pages I have already written. There's a great lot of them, and I think there's apt to be a great lot more before I am through. "That Alzheimer's, do you know what it really is?"

"No," I said, "but I'm sure you'll tell me, Brad."

"It's AIDS for old people," he said, and then burst out laughing, hucka-hucka-hucka-*huck*!, just like he does over those idiotic jokes of his.

I didn't laugh, though, because what he said struck

a nerve somewhere. Not that I have Alzheimer's; although there's plenty of it on view here at beautiful Georgia Pines, I myself just suffer the standard old-guy memory problems. Those problems seem to have more to do with *when* than *what*. Looking over what I have written so far, it occurs to me that I *remember* everything that happened back in '32; it's the order of events that sometimes gets confused in my head. Yet, if I'm careful, I think I can keep even that sorted out. More or less.

John Coffey came to E Block and the Green Mile in October of that year, condemned for the murder of the nine-year-old Detterick twins. That's my major landmark, and if I keep it in view, I should do just fine. William "Wild Bill" Wharton came after Coffey; Delacroix came before. So did the mouse, the one Brutus Howell—Brutal, to his friends—called Steamboat Willy and Delacroix ended up calling Mr. Jingles.

Whatever you called him, the mouse came first, even before Del—it was still summer when he showed up, and we had two other prisoners on the Green Mile: The Chief, Arlen Bitterbuck; and The Pres, Arthur Flanders.

That mouse. That goddam mouse. Delacroix loved it, but Percy Wetmore sure didn't.

Percy hated it from the first.

2

The mouse came back just about three days after Percy had chased it down the Green Mile that first time. Dean Stanton and Bill Dodge were talking politics . . . which meant, in those days, they were talking Roosevelt and Hoover—Herbert, not J. Edgar. They were eating Ritz crackers from a box Dean had purchased from old Toot-Toot an hour or so before. Percy was standing in the office doorway, practicing quick draws with the baton he loved so much, as he listened. He'd pull it out of that ridiculous hand-tooled holster he'd gotten somewhere, then twirl it (or try to; most times he would have dropped it if not for the rawhide loop he kept on his wrist), then re-holster it. I was off that night, but got the full report from Dean the following evening.

The mouse came up the Green Mile just as it had before, hopping along, then stopping and seeming to check the empty cells. After a bit of that it would hop on, undiscouraged, as if it had known all along it would be a long search, and it was up to that.

The President was awake this time, standing at his cell door. That guy was a piece of work, managing to look natty even in his prison blues. We knew just by the way he looked that he wasn't made for Old Sparky, and we were right—less than a week after Percy's second run at that mouse, The Pres's sentence was commuted to life and he joined the general population.

"Say!" he called. "There's a mouse in here! What kind of a joint are you guys running, anyway?" He was kind of laughing, but Dean said he also sounded kind of outraged, as if even a murder rap hadn't been quite enough to knock the Kiwanis out of his soul. He had been the regional head of an outfit called Mid-South Realty Associates, and had thought himself smart enough to be able to get away with pushing his half-senile father out a third-story window and collect on a double-indemnity whole-life policy. On that he had been wrong, but maybe not by much.

"Shut up, you lugoon," Percy said, but that was pretty much automatic. He had his eye on the mouse. He had re-holstered his baton and taken out one of his magazines, but now he tossed the magazine on the duty desk and pulled the baton out of its holster again. He began tapping it casually against the knuckles of his left hand.

"Son of a bitch," Bill Dodge said. "I've never seen a mouse in here before."

"Aw, he's sort of cute," Dean said. "And not afraid at all."

"How do you know?"

"He was in the other night. Percy saw him, too. Brutal calls him Steamboat Willy."

Percy kind of sneered at that, but for the time being said nothing. He was tapping the baton faster now on the back of his hand.

"Watch this," Dean said. "He came all the way up to the desk before. I want to see if he'll do it again."

It did, skirting wide of The Pres on its way, as if it didn't like the way our resident parricide smelled. It checked two of the empty cells, even ran up onto one of the bare, unmattressed cots for a sniff, then came back to the Green Mile. And Percy standing there the whole time, tapping and tapping, not talking for a change, wanting to make it sorry for coming back. Wanting to teach it a lesson.

"Good thing you guys don't have to put him in Sparky," Bill said, interested in spite of himself. "You'd have a hell of a time getting the clamps and the cap on."

Percy said nothing still, but he very slowly gripped the baton between his fingers, the way a man would hold a good cigar.

The mouse stopped where it had before, no more than three feet from the duty desk, looking up at Dean like a prisoner before the bar. It glanced up at Bill for a moment, then switched its attention back to Dean. Percy it hardly seemed to notice at all.

"He's a brave little barstid, I got to give him that," Bill said. He raised his voice a little. "Hey! Hey! Steamboat Willy!"

The mouse flinched a little and fluttered its ears, but it didn't run, or even show any signs of wanting to.

"Now watch this," Dean said, remembering how Brutal had fed it some of his corned-beef sandwich. "I don't know if he'll do it again, but—"

He broke off a piece of Ritz cracker and dropped it in front of the mouse. It just looked with its sharp black eyes at the orangey fragment for a second or two, its filament-fine whiskers twitching as it sniffed. Then it reached out, took the cracker in its paws, sat up, and began to eat.

"Well, I'll be shucked and boiled!" Bill exclaimed. "Eats as neat as a parson on parish house Saturday night!"

"Looks more like a nigger eating watermelon to me," Percy remarked, but neither guard paid him any mind. Neither did The Chief or The Pres, for that matter. The mouse finished the cracker but continued to sit, seemingly balanced on the talented coil of its tail, looking up at the giants in blue.

"Lemme try," Bill said. He broke off another piece of cracker, leaned over the front of the desk, and dropped it carefully. The mouse sniffed but did not touch.

"Huh," Bill said. "Must be full."

"Nah," Dean said, "he knows you're a floater, that's all."

"Floater, am I? I like that! I'm here almost as much as Harry Terwilliger! Maybe more!"

"Simmer down, old-timer, simmer down," Dean said, grinning. "But watch and see if I'm not right." He bombed another piece of cracker over the side. Sure enough, the mouse picked that one up and began to eat again, still ignoring Bill Dodge's contribution completely. But before it had done more than take a preliminary nibble or two, Percy threw his baton at it, launching it like a spear.

The mouse was a small target, and give the devil his due—it was a wickedly good shot, and might have taken "Willy's" head clean off, if its reflexes hadn't been as sharp as shards of broken glass. It ducked—yes, just as a human being would have—and dropped the chunk of cracker. The heavy hickory baton passed over its head and spine close enough so its fur ruffled (that's what Dean said, anyway, and so I pass it on, although I'm not sure I really believe it), then hit the green linoleum and bounced against the bars of an empty cell. The mouse didn't wait to see if it was a mistake; apparently remembering a pressing engagement elsewhere, it turned and was off down the corridor toward the restraint room in a flash.

Percy roared with frustration—he knew how close he had come—and chased after it again. Bill Dodge grabbed at his arm, probably out of simple instinct, but Percy pulled away from him. Still, Dean said, it was probably that grab which saved Steamboat Willy's life, and it was still a near thing. Percy wanted not just to kill the mouse but to *squash* it, so he ran in big, comical leaps, like a deer, stamping down with his heavy black workshoes. The mouse barely avoided Percy's last two jumps, first zigging and then zagging. It went under the door with a final flick of its long pink tail, and so long, stranger—it was gone.

"Fuck!" Percy said, and slammed the flat of his hand against the door. Then he began to sort through his keys, meaning to go into the restraint room and continue the chase.

Dean came down the corridor after him, deliberately walking slow in order to get his emotions under control. Part of him wanted to laugh at Percy, he told me, but part of him wanted to grab the man, whirl him around, pin him against the restraint-room door, and whale the living daylights out of him. Most of it, of course, was just being startled; our job on E Block was to keep rumpus to a minimum, and rumpus was practically Percy Wetmore's middle name. Working with him was sort of like trying to defuse a bomb with somebody standing behind you and every now and then clashing a pair of cymbals together. In a word, upsetting. Dean said he could see that upset in Arlen Bitterbuck's eyes . . . even in The President's eyes, although that gentleman was usually as cool as the storied cucumber.

And there was something else, as well. In some part of his mind, Dean had already begun to accept the mouse as—well, maybe not as a friend, but as a part of life on the block. That made what Percy had done and what he was trying to do not right. Not even if it was a mouse he was trying to do it to. And the fact that Percy would never understand how come it wasn't right was pretty much the perfect example of why he was all wrong for the job he thought he was doing.

By the time Dean reached the end of the corridor, he had gotten himself under control again, and knew how he wanted to handle the matter. The one thing Percy absolutely couldn't stand was to look foolish, and we all knew it.

"Coises, foiled again," he said, grinning a little, kidding Percy along.

Percy gave him an ugly look and flicked his hair off his brow. "Watch your mouth, Four-Eyes. I'm riled. Don't make it worse."

"So it's moving day again, is it?" Dean said, not quite laughing . . . but laughing with his eyes. "Well, when you get everything out this time, would you mind mopping the floor?"

Percy looked at the door. Looked at his keys. Thought about another long, hot, fruitless rummage in the room with the soft walls while they all stood around and watched him . . . The Chief and The Pres, too.

"I'll be damned if I understand what's so funny,"

he said. "We don't need mice in the cellblock—we got enough vermin in here already, without adding mice."

"Whatever you say, Percy," Dean said, holding up his hands. He had a moment right there, he told me the next night, when he believed Percy might just take after him.

Bill Dodge strolled up then and smoothed it over. "Think you dropped this," he said, and handed Percy his baton. "An inch lower, you woulda broken the little barstid's back."

Percy's chest expanded at that. "Yeah, it wasn't a bad shot," he said, carefully re-seating his head-knocker in its foolish holster. "I used to be a pitcher in high school. Threw two no-hitters."

"Is that right, now?" Bill said, and the respectful tone of voice (although he winked at Dean when Percy turned away) was enough to finish defusing the situation.

"Yep," Percy said. "Threw one down in Knoxville. Those city boys didn't know what hit em. Walked two. Could have had a perfect game if the ump hadn't been such a lugoon."

Dean could have left it at that, but he had seniority on Percy, and part of a senior's job is to instruct, and at that time—before Coffey, before Delacroix—he still thought Percy might be teachable. So he reached out and grasped the younger man's wrist. "You want to think about what you was doing just now," Dean said. His intention, he said later, was to sound serious but not disapproving. Not *too* disapproving, anyway.

Except with Percy, that didn't work. He might not learn . . . but we would eventually.

"Say, Four-Eyes, I know what I was doing—trying to get that mouse! What're you, blind?"

"You also scared the cheese out of Bill, out of me, and out of them," Dean said, pointing in the direction of Bitterbuck and Flanders.

"So what?" Percy asked, drawing himself up. "They ain't in cradle-school, in case you didn't notice. Although you guys treat them that way half the time."

"Well, *I* don't like to be scared," Bill rumbled, "and I work here, Wetmore, in case you didn't notice. *I* ain't one of your lugoons."

Percy gave him a look that was narrow-eyed and a touch uncertain.

"And we don't scare them any more than we have to, because they're under a lot of strain," Dean said. He was still keeping his voice low. "Men that are under a lot of strain can snap. Hurt themselves. Hurt others. Sometimes get folks like us in trouble, too."

Percy's mouth twitched at that. "In trouble" was an idea that had power over him. Making trouble was okay. Getting into it was not.

"Our job is talking, not yelling," Dean said. "A man who is yelling at prisoners is a man who has lost control."

Percy knew who had written that scripture—me.

The boss. There was no love lost between Percy Wetmore and Paul Edgecombe, and this was still summer, remember—long before the real festivities started.

"You'll do better," Dean said, "if you think of this place as like an intensive-care ward in a hospital. It's best to be quiet—"

"I think of it as a bucket of piss to drown rats in," Percy said, "and that's all. Now let me go."

He tore free of Dean's hand, stepped between him and Bill, and stalked up the corridor with his head down. He walked a little too close to The President's side—close enough so that Flanders could have reached out, grabbed him, and maybe headwhipped him with his own prized hickory baton, had Flanders been that sort of man. He wasn't, of course, but The Chief perhaps was. The Chief, if given a chance, might have administered such a beating just to teach Percy a lesson. What Dean said to me on that subject when he told me this story the following night has stuck with me ever since, because it turned out to be a kind of prophecy. "Wetmore don't understand that he hasn't got any power over them," Dean said. "That nothing he does can really make things worse for them, that they can only be electrocuted once. Until he gets his head around that, he's going to be a danger to himself and to everyone else down here."

Percy went into my office and slammed the door behind him.

"My, my," Bill Dodge said. "Ain't he the swollen and badly infected testicle."

"You don't know the half of it," Dean said.

"Oh, look on the bright side," Bill said. He was always telling people to look on the bright side; it got so you wanted to punch his nose every time it came out of his mouth. "Your trick mouse got away, at least."

"Yeah, but we won't see him no more," Dean said. "I imagine this time goddam Percy Wetmore's scared him off for good."

3

That was logical but wrong. The mouse was back the very next evening, which just happened to be the first of Percy Wetmore's two nights off before he slid over to the graveyard shift.

Steamboat Willy showed up around seven o'clock. I was there to see his reappearance; so was Dean. Harry Terwilliger, too. Harry was on the desk. I was technically on days, but had stuck around to spend an extra hour with The Chief, whose time was getting close by then. Bitterbuck was stoical on the outside, in the tradition of his tribe, but I could see his fear of the end growing inside him like a poison flower. So we talked. You could talk to them in the daytime but it wasn't so good, with the shouts and conversation (not to mention the occasional fist-fight) coming from the exercise yard, the chonk-chonk-chonk of the stamping machines in the plate-shop, the occasional yell of a guard for someone to put down that pick or grab up that hoe or just to get your ass over here, Harvey. After four it got a little better, and after six it got better still. Six to eight was the optimum time. After that you could see the long thoughts starting to steal over their minds again—in their eyes you could see it, like afternoon shadows—and it was best to stop. They still heard what you were saying, but it no longer made sense to them. Past eight they were getting ready for the watches of the night and imagining how the cap would feel when it was clamped to the tops of their heads, and how the air would smell inside the black bag which had been rolled down over their sweaty faces.

But I got The Chief at a good time. He told me about his first wife, and how they had built a lodge together up in Montana. Those had been the happiest days of his life, he said. The water was so pure and so cold that it felt like your mouth was cut every time you drank.

"Hey, Mr. Edgecombe," he said. "You think, if a man he sincerely repent of what he done wrong, he might get to go back to the time that was happiest for him and live there forever? Could that be what heaven is like?"

"I've just about believed that very thing," I said, which was a lie I didn't regret in the least. I had learned of matters eternal at my mother's pretty knee, and what I believed is what the Good Book says about murderers: that there is no eternal life in them. I think they go straight to hell, where they burn in torment until God finally gives Gabriel the nod to blow the Judgment Trump. When he does, they'll wink out . . . and probably glad to go they will be. But I never gave a hint of such beliefs to Bitterbuck, or to any of them. I think in their hearts they knew it. *Where is your brother, his blood crieth to me from the ground*, God said to Cain, and I doubt if the words were much of a surprise to that particular problem-child; I bet he heard Abel's blood whining out of the earth at him with each step he took.

The Chief was smiling when I left, perhaps thinking about his lodge in Montana and his wife lying bare-breasted in the light of the fire. He would be walking in a warmer fire soon, I had no doubt.

I went back up the corridor, and Dean told me about his set-to with Percy the previous night. I think he'd waited around just so he could, and I listened carefully. I always listened carefully when the subject was Percy, because I agreed with Dean a hundred per cent—I thought Percy was the sort of man who could cause a lot of trouble, as much for the rest of us as for himself.

As Dean was finishing, old Toot-Toot came by with his red snack-wagon, which was covered with hand-lettered Bible quotes ("REPENT for the LORD shall judge his people," Deut. 32:36, "And surely your BLOOD of your lives will I require," Gen. 9:5, and similar cheery, uplifting sentiments), and sold us some sandwiches and pops. Dean was hunting for change in his pocket and saying that we wouldn't see Steamboat Willy anymore, that goddam Percy Wetmore had scared him off for good, when old Toot-Toot said, "What's that'ere, then?"

We looked, and here came the mouse of the hour his ownself, hopping up the middle of the Green Mile. He'd come a little way, then stop, look around with his bright little oildrop eyes, then come on again.

"Hey, mouse!" The Chief said, and the mouse stopped and looked at him, whiskers twitching. I tell you, it was exactly as if the damned thing knew it had been called. "You some kind of spirit guide?" Bitterbuck tossed the mouse a little morsel of cheese from his supper. It landed right in front of the mouse, but Steamboat Willy hardly even glanced at it, just came on his way again, up the Green Mile, looking in empty cells.

"Boss Edgecombe!" The President called. "Do you think that little bastard knows Wetmore isn't here? I do, by God!"

I felt about the same . . . but I wasn't going to say so out loud.

Harry came out into the hall, hitching up his pants the way he always did after he'd spent a refreshing few minutes in the can, and stood there with his eyes wide. Toot-Toot was also staring, a sunken grin doing unpleasant things to the soft and toothless lower half of his face.

The mouse stopped in what was becoming its usual spot, curled its tail around its paws, and looked at us. Again I was reminded of pictures I had seen of judges passing sentence on hapless prisoners ... yet, had there ever been a prisoner as small and unafraid as this one? Not that it really was a prisoner, of course; it could come and go pretty much as it pleased. Yet the idea would not leave my mind, and it again occurred to me that most of us would feel that small when approaching God's judgment seat after our lives were over, but very few of us would be able to look so unafraid.

"Well, I swear," Old Toot-Toot said. "There he sits, big as Billy-Be-Frigged."

"You ain't seen nothing yet, Toot," Harry said. "Watch this." He reached into his breast pocket and came out with a slice of cinnamon apple wrapped in waxed paper. He broke off the end and tossed it on the floor. It was dry and hard and I thought it would bounce right past the mouse, but it reached out one paw, as carelessly as a man swatting at a fly to pass the time, and batted it flat. We all laughed in admiration and surprise, an outburst of sound that should have sent the mouse skittering, but it barely twitched. It picked up the piece of dried apple in its paws, gave it a couple of licks, then dropped it and looked up at us as if to say, Not bad, what else do you have?

Toot-Toot opened his cart, took out a sandwich, unwrapped it, and tore off a scrap of bologna.

"Don't bother," Dean said.

"What do you mean?" Toot-Toot asked. "Ain't a

mouse alive'd pass up bologna if he could get it. You a crazy guy!"

But I knew Dean was right, and I could see by Harry's face that he knew it, too. There were floaters and there were regulars. Somehow, that mouse seemed to know the difference. Nuts, but true.

Old Toot-Toot tossed the scrap of bologna down, and sure enough, the mouse wouldn't have a thing to do with it; sniffed it once and then backed off a pace.

"I'll be a goddamned son of a bitch," Old Toot-Toot said, sounding offended.

I held out my hand. "Give it to me."

"What—same sammitch?"

"Same one. I'll pay for it."

Toot-Toot handed it over. I lifted the top slice of bread, tore off another sliver of meat, and dropped it over the front of the duty desk. The mouse came forward at once, picked it up in its paws, and began to eat. The bologna was gone before you could say Jack Robinson.

"I'll be *goddamned*!" Toot-Toot cried. "Bloody hell! Gimme dat!"

He snatched back the sandwich, tore off a much larger piece of meat—not a scrap this time but a flap—and dropped it so close to the mouse that Steamboat Willy almost ended up wearing it for a hat. It drew back again, sniffed (surely no mouse ever hit such a jackpot during the Depression—not in *our* state, at least), and then looked up at us.

"Go on, eat it!" Toot-Toot said, sounding more of-fended than ever. "What's wrong witchoo?"

Dean took the sandwich and dropped a piece of meat—by then it was like some strange communion service. The mouse picked it up at once and bolted it down. Then it turned and went back down the corri-dor to the restraint room, pausing along the way to peer into a couple of empty cells and to take a brief investigatory tour of a third. Once again the idea that it was looking for someone occurred to me, and this time I dismissed the thought more slowly.

"I'm not going to talk about this," Harry said. He sounded as if he was half-joking, half-not. "First of all, nobody'd care. Second, they wouldn't believe me if they did."

"He only ate from you fellas," Toot-Toot said. He shook his head in disbelief, then bent laboriously over, picked up what the mouse had disdained, and popped it into his own toothless maw, where he be-gan the job of gumming it into submission. "Now why he do dat?"

"I've got a better one," Harry said. "How'd he know Percy was off?"

"He didn't," I said. "It was just coincidence, that mouse showing up tonight."

Except that got harder and harder to believe as the days went by and the mouse showed up only when Percy was off, on another shift, or in another part of the prison. We—Harry, Dean, Brutal, and me—decided that it must know Percy's voice, or his smell.

We carefully avoided too much discussion about the mouse itself—*himself*. That, we seemed to have decided without saying a word, might go a long way toward spoiling something that was special ... and beautiful, by virtue of its strangeness and delicacy. Willy had chosen us, after all, in some way I do not understand, even now. Maybe Harry came closest when he said it would do no good to tell other people, not just because they wouldn't believe but because they wouldn't care.

4

Then it was time for the execution of Arlen Bitterbuck, in reality no chief but first elder of his tribe on the Washita Reservation, and a member of the Cherokee Council as well. He had killed a man while drunk—while both of them were drunk, in fact. The Chief had crushed the man's head with a cement block. At issue had been a pair of boots. So, on July seventeenth of that rainy summer, *my* council of elders intended for his life to end.

Visiting hours for most Cold Mountain prisoners were as rigid as steel beams, but that didn't hold for our boys on E Block. So, on the sixteenth, Bitterbuck was allowed over to the long room adjacent to the cafeteria—the Arcade. It was divided straight down the middle by mesh interwoven with strands of barbed wire. Here The Chief would visit with his second wife and those of his children who would still treat with him. It was time for the good-byes.

He was taken over there by Bill Dodge and two other floaters. The rest of us had work to do—one hour to cram in at least two rehearsals. Three if we could manage it.

Percy didn't make much protest over being put in the switch room with Jack Van Hay for the Bitterbuck electrocution; he was too green to know if he was being given a good spot or a bad one. What he did know was that he had a rectangular mesh window to look through, and although he probably didn't care to be looking at the back of the chair instead of the front, he would still be close enough to see the sparks flying.

Right outside that window was a black wall telephone with no crank or dial on it. That phone could only ring in, and only from one place: the governor's office. I've seen lots of jailhouse movies over the years where the official phone rings just as they're getting ready to pull the switch on some poor innocent sap, but ours never rang during all my years on E Block, never once. In the movies, salvation is cheap. So is innocence. You pay a quarter, and a quarter's worth is just what you get. Real life costs more, and most of the answers are different.

We had a tailor's dummy down in the tunnel for the run to the meatwagon, and we had Old Toot-Toot for the rest. Over the years, Toot had somehow become the traditional stand-in for the condemned, as time-honored in his way as the goose you sit down to on Christmas, whether you like goose or not. Most of the other screws liked him, were amused by his funny accent—also French, but Canadian rather than

Cajun, and softened into its own thing by his years of incarceration in the South. Even Brutal got a kick out of Old Toot. Not me, though. I thought he was, in his way, an older and dimmer version of Percy Wetmore, a man too squeamish to kill and cook his own meat but who did, all the same, just *love* the smell of a barbecue.

We were all there for the rehearsal, just as we would all be there for the main event. Brutus Howell had been "put out," as we said, which meant that he would place the cap, monitor the governor's phoneline, summon the doctor from his place by the wall if he was needed, and give the actual order to roll on two when the time came. If it went well, there would be no credit for anyone. If it didn't go well, Brutal would be blamed by the witnesses and I would be blamed by the warden. Neither of us complained about this; it wouldn't have done any good. The world turns, that's all. You can hold on and turn with it, or stand up to protest and be spun right off.

Dean, Harry Terwilliger, and I walked down to The Chief's cell for the first rehearsal not three minutes after Bill and his troops had escorted Bitterbuck off the block and over to the Arcade. The cell door was open, and Old Toot-Toot sat on The Chief's bunk, his wispy white hair flying.

"There come-stains all over dis sheet," Toot-Toot remarked. "He mus' be tryin to get rid of it before you fellas boil it off." And he cackled.

"Shut up, Toot," Dean said. "Let's play this serious."

"Okay," Toot-Toot said, immediately composing his face into an expression of thunderous gravity. But his eyes twinkled. Old Toot never looked so alive as when he was playing dead.

I stepped forward. "Arlen Bitterbuck, as an officer of the court and of the state of blah-blah, I have a warrant for blah-blah, such execution to be carried out at twelve-oh-one on blah-blah, will you step forward?"

Toot got off the bunk. "I'm steppin forward, I'm steppin forward, I'm steppin forward," he said.

"Turn around," Dean said, and when Toot-Toot turned, Dean examined the dandruffy top of his head. The crown of The Chief's head would be shaved tomorrow night, and Dean's check then would be to make sure he didn't need a touch-up. Stubble could impede conduction, make things harder. Everything we were doing today was about making things easier.

"All right, Arlen, let's go," I said to Toot-Toot, and away we went.

"I'm walkin down the corridor, I'm walkin down the corridor, I'm walkin down the corridor," Toot said. I flanked him on the left, Dean on the right. Harry was directly behind him. At the head of the corridor we turned right, away from life as it was lived in the exercise yard and toward death as it was died in the storage room. We went into my office, and Toot dropped to his knees without having to be asked. He knew the script, all right, probably better than any of us. God knew he'd been there longer than any of us.

"I'm prayin, I'm prayin, I'm prayin," Toot-Toot said, holding his gnarled hands up. They looked like that famous engraving, you probably know the one I mean. "The Lord is my shepherd, so on n so forth."

"Who's Bitterbuck got?" Harry asked. "We're not going to have some Cherokee medicine man in here shaking his dick, are we?"

"Actually—"

"Still prayin, still prayin, still gettin right with Jesus," Toot overrode me.

"Shut up, you old gink," Dean said.

"I'm prayin!"

"Then pray to yourself."

"What's keepin you guys?" Brutal hollered in from the storage room. That had also been emptied for our use. We were in the killing zone again, all right; it was a thing you could almost smell.

"Hold your friggin water!" Harry yelled back. "Don't be so goddam impatient!"

"Prayin," Toot said, grinning his unpleasant sunken grin. "Prayin for patience, just a little goddam patience."

"Actually, Bitterbuck's a Christian—he says," I told them, "and he's perfectly happy with the Baptist guy who came for Tillman Clark. Schuster, his name is. I like him, too. He's fast, and he doesn't get them all worked up. On your feet, Toot. You prayed enough for one day."

"Walkin," Toot said. "Walkin again, walkin again, yes sir, walkin on the Green Mile."

Short as he was, he still had to duck a little to get through the door on the far side of the office. The rest of us had to duck even more. This was a vulnerable time with a real prisoner, and when I looked across to the platform where Old Sparky stood and saw Brutal with his gun drawn, I nodded with satisfaction. Just right.

Toot-Toot went down the steps and stopped. The folding wooden chairs, about forty of them, were already in place. Bitterbuck would cross to the platform on an angle that would keep him safely away from the seated spectators, and half a dozen guards would be added for insurance. Bill Dodge would be in charge of those. We had never had a witness menaced by a condemned prisoner in spite of what was, admittedly, a raw set-up . . . and that was how I meant to keep it.

"Ready, boys?" Toot asked when we were back in our original formation at the foot of the stairs leading down from my office. I nodded, and we walked to the platform. What we looked like more than anything, I often thought, was a color-guard that had forgotten its flag.

"What am *I* supposed to do?" Percy called from behind the wire mesh between the storage room and the switch room.

"Watch and learn," I called back.

"And keep yer hands off yer wiener," Harry muttered. Toot-Toot heard him, though, and cackled.

We escorted him up onto the platform and Toot turned around on his own—the old vet in action. "Sittin down," he said, "sittin down, sittin down, takin a seat in Old Sparky's lap."

I dropped to my right knee before his right leg. Dean dropped to his left knee before his left leg. It was at this point we ourselves would be most vulnerable to physical attack, should the condemned man go berserk . . . which, every now and then, they did. We both turned the cocked knee slightly inward, to protect the crotch area. We dropped our chins to protect our throats. And, of course, we moved to secure the ankles and neutralize the danger as fast as we could. The Chief would be wearing slippers when he took his final promenade, but "it could have been worse" isn't much comfort to a man with a ruptured larynx. Or writhing on the floor with his balls swelling up to the size of Mason jars, for that matter, while forty or so spectators—many of them gentlemen of the press—sit in those Grange-hall chairs, watching the whole thing.

We clamped Toot-Toot's ankles. The clamp on Dean's side was slightly bigger, because it carried the juice. When Bitterbuck sat down tomorrow night, he would do so with a shaved left calf. Indians have very little body-hair as a rule, but we would take no chances.

While we were clamping Toot-Toot's ankles, Brutal secured his right wrist. Harry stepped smoothly forward and clamped the left. When they were done, Harry nodded to Brutal, and Brutal called back to Van Hay: "Roll on one!"

I heard Percy asking Jack Van Hay what that meant (it was hard to believe how little he knew, how little he'd picked up during his time on E Block) and Van Hay's murmur of explanation. Today *Roll on one* meant nothing, but when he heard Brutal say it tomorrow night, Van Hay would turn the knob that goosed the prison generator behind B Block. The witnesses would hear the genny as a steady low humming, and the lights all over the prison would brighten. In the other cellblocks, prisoners would observe those overbright lights and think it had happened, the execution was over, when in fact it was just beginning.

Brutal stepped around the chair so that Toot could see him. "Arlen Bitterbuck, you have been condemned to die in the electric chair, sentence passed by a jury of your peers and imposed by a judge in good standing in this state. God save the people of this state. Do you have anything to say before sentence is carried out?"

"Yeah," Toot said, eyes gleaming, lips bunched in a toothless happy grin. "I want a fried chicken dinner with gravy on the taters, I want to shit in your hat, and I got to have Mae West sit on my face, because I am one horny motherfucker."

Brutal tried to hold onto his stern expression, but it was impossible. He threw back his head and began laughing. Dean collapsed onto the edge of the platform like he'd been gutshot, head down between his knees, howling like a coyote, with one hand clapped to his brow as if to keep his brains in there where they belonged. Harry was knocking his own head against the wall and going *huh-huh-huh* as if he had a glob of food stuck in his throat. Even Jack Van Hay, a man not known for his sense of humor, was laughing. I felt like it myself, of course I did, but controlled it somehow. Tomorrow night it was going to be for real, and a man would die there where Toot-Toot was sitting.

"Shut up, Brutal," I said. "You too, Dean. Harry. And Toot, the next remark like that to come out of your mouth will be your last. I'll have Van Hay roll on two for real."

Toot gave me a grin as if to say that was a good 'un, Boss Edgecombe, a real good 'un. It faltered into a narrow, puzzled look when he saw I wasn't answering it. "What's wrong witchoo?" he asked.

"It's not funny," I said. "That's what's wrong with me, and if you're not smart enough to get it, you better just keep your gob shut." Except it *was* funny, in its way, and I suppose that was what had really made me mad.

I looked around, saw Brutal staring at me, still grinning a little.

"Shit," I said, "I'm getting too old for this job."

"Nah," Brutal said. "You're in your prime, Paul." But I wasn't, neither was he, not as far as this goddam job went, and both of us knew it. Still, the important thing was that the laughing fit had passed. That was good, because the last thing I wanted was somebody remembering Toot's smart-aleck remark tomorrow night and getting going again. You'd say such a thing would be impossible, a guard laughing his ass off as he escorted a condemned man past the witnesses to the electric chair, but when men are under stress, *anything* can happen. And a thing like that, people would have talked about it for twenty years.

"Are you going to be quiet, Toot?" I asked.

"Yes," he said, his averted face that of the world's oldest, poutiest child.

I nodded to Brutal that he should get on with the rehearsal. He took the mask from the brass hook on the back of the chair and rolled it down over Toot-Toot's head, pulling it snug under his chin, which opened the hole at the top to its widest diameter. Then Brutal leaned over, picked the wet circle of sponge out of the bucket, pressed one finger against it, then licked the tip of the finger. That done, he put the sponge back in the bucket. Tomorrow he wouldn't. Tomorrow he would tuck it into the cap perched on the back of the chair. Not today, though; there was no need to get Toot's old head wet.

The cap was steel, and with the straps dangling down on either side, it looked sort of like a doughboy's helmet. Brutal put it on Old Toot-Toot's head, snugging it down over the hole in the black head-covering.

"Gettin the cap, gettin the cap, gettin the cap," Toot said, and now his voice sounded squeezed as well as muffled. The straps held his jaw almost closed, and I suspected Brutal had snugged it down a little tighter than he strictly had to for purposes of rehearsal. He stepped back, faced the empty seats, and said: "Arlen Bitterbuck, electricity shall now be passed through your body until you are dead, in accordance with state law. May God have mercy on your soul."

Brutal turned to the mesh-covered rectangle. "Roll on two."

Old Toot, perhaps trying to recapture his earlier flare of comic genius, began to buck and flail in the chair, as Old Sparky's actual customers almost never did. "Now I'm fryin!" he cried. "Fryin! Fryyyin! *Geeeaah!* I'm a done tom turkey!"

Harry and Dean, I saw, were not watching this at all. They had turned away from Sparky and were looking across the empty storage room at the door leading back into my office. "Well, I'll be god-damned," Harry said. "One of the witnesses came a day early."

Sitting in the doorway with its tail curled neatly around its paws, watching with its beady black oilspot eyes, was the mouse.

5

The execution went well—if there was ever such a thing as "a good one" (a proposition I strongly doubt), then the execution of Arlen Bitterbuck, council elder of the Washita Cherokee, was it. He got his braids wrong—his hands were shaking too badly to make a good job of it—and his eldest daughter, a woman of thirty-odd, was allowed to plait them nice and even. She wanted to weave feathers in at the tips, the pinfeathers of a hawk, his bird, but I couldn't allow it. They might catch fire and burn. I didn't tell her that, of course, just said it was against regulations. She made no protest, only bowed her head and put her hands to her temples to show her disappointment and her disapproval. She conducted herself with great dignity, that woman, and by doing so practically guaranteed that her father would do the same.

The Chief left his cell with no protest or holding back when the time came. Sometimes we had to pry their fingers off the bars—I broke one or two in my time and have never forgotten the muffled snapping sound—but The Chief wasn't one of those, thank God. He walked strong up the Green Mile to my office, and there he dropped to his knees to pray with Brother Schuster, who had driven down from the Heavenly Light Baptist Church in his flivver. Schuster gave The Chief a few psalms, and The Chief started to cry when Schuster got to the one about lying down beside the still waters. It wasn't bad, though, no hysteria, nothing like that. I had an idea he was thinking about still water so pure and so cold it felt like it was cutting your mouth every time you drank some.

Actually, I like to see them cry a little. It's when they don't that I get worried.

A lot of men can't get up from their knees again without help, but The Chief did okay in that department. He swayed a little at first, like he was light-headed, and Dean put out a hand to steady him, but Bitterbuck had already found his balance again on his own, so out we went.

Almost all the chairs were occupied, with the people in them murmuring quietly among themselves, like folks do when they're waiting for a wedding or a funeral to get started. That was the only time Bitterbuck faltered. I don't know if it was any one person in particular that bothered him, or all of them together, but I could hear a low moaning start up in his throat, and all at once the arm I was holding had a drag in it that hadn't been there before. Out of the corner of my eye I could see Harry Terwilliger moving up to cut off The Chief's retreat if Bitterbuck all at once decided he wanted to go hard.

I tightened my grip on his elbow and tapped the inside of his arm with one finger. "Steady, Chief," I said out of the corner of my mouth, not moving my lips. "The only thing most of these people will remember about you is how you go out, so give them something good—show them how a Washita does it."

He glanced at me sideways and gave a little nod. Then he took one of the braids his daughter had made and kissed it. I looked to Brutal, standing at parade rest behind the chair, resplendent in his best blue uniform, all the buttons on the tunic polished and gleaming, his hat sitting square-john perfect on his big head. I gave him a little nod and he shot it right back, stepping forward to help Bitterbuck mount the platform if he needed help. Turned out he didn't.

It was less than a minute from the time Bitterbuck sat down in the chair to the moment when Brutal called "Roll on two!" softly back over his shoulder. The lights dimmed down again, but only a little; you wouldn't have noticed it if you hadn't been looking for it. That meant Van Hay had pulled the switch some wit had labeled MABEL'S HAIR DRIER. There was a low humming from the cap, and Bitterbuck surged forward against the clamps and the restraining belt across his chest. Over against the wall, the prison doctor watched expressionlessly, lips thinned down until his mouth looked like a single white stitch. There was no flopping and flailing, such as Old Toot-Toot had done at rehearsal, only that powerful forward surge, as a man may surge forward from the hips while in the grip of a powerful orgasm. The Chief's blue shirt pulled tight at the buttons, creating little strained smiles of flesh between them.

And there was a smell. Not bad in itself, but unpleasant in its associations. I've never been able to go down in the cellar at my granddaughter's house when they bring me there, although that's where their little boy has his Lionel set-up, which he would dearly love to share with his great-grampa. I don't mind the trains, as I'm sure you can guess—it's the transformer I can't abide. The way it hums. And the way, when it gets hot, it *smells*. Even after all these years, that smell reminds me of Cold Mountain.

Van Hay gave him thirty seconds, then turned the juice off. The doctor stepped forward from his place and listened with his stethoscope. There was no talk from the witnesses now. The doctor straightened up and looked through the mesh. "Disorganized," he said, and made a twirling, cranking gesture with one finger. He had heard a few random heartbeats from Bitterbuck's chest, probably as meaningless as the final jitters of a decapitated chicken, but it was better not to take chances. You didn't want him suddenly sitting up on the gurney when you had him halfway through the tunnel, bawling that he felt like he was on fire.

Van Hay rolled on three and The Chief surged forward again, twisting a little from side to side in the grip of the current. When doc listened this time, he nodded. It was over. We had once again succeeded in destroying what we could not create. Some of the folks in the audience had begun talking in those low voices again; most sat with their heads down, looking at the floor, as if stunned. Or ashamed.

Harry and Dean came up with the stretcher. It was actually Percy's job to take one end, but he didn't know and no one had bothered to tell him. The Chief, still wearing the black silk hood, was loaded onto it by Brutal and me, and we whisked him through the door which led to the tunnel as fast as we could manage it without actually running. Smoke—too much of it—was rising from the hole in the top of the mask, and there was a horrible stench.

"Aw, man!" Percy cried, his voice wavering. "What's that smell?"

"Just get out of my way and stay out of it," Brutal said, shoving past him to get to the wall where there was a mounted fire extinguisher. It was one of the old chemical kind that you had to pump. Dean, meanwhile, had stripped off the hood. It wasn't as bad as it could have been; Bitterbuck's left braid was smouldering like a pile of wet leaves.

"Never mind that thing," I told Brutal. I didn't want to have to clean a load of chemical slime off the dead man's face before putting him in the back of the meatwagon. I slapped at The Chief's head (Percy staring at me, wide-eyed, the whole time) until the smoke quit rising. Then we carried the body down the twelve wooden steps to the tunnel. Here it was as chilly and dank as a dungeon, with the hollow plink-plink sound of dripping water. Hanging lights with crude tin shades—they were made in the prison machine-shop—showed a brick tube that ran thirty feet under the highway. The top was curved and wet. It made me feel like a character in an Edgar Allan Poe story every time I used it.

There was a gurney waiting. We loaded Bitterbuck's body onto it, and I made a final check to make sure his hair was out. That one braid was pretty well charred, and I was sorry to see that the cunning little bow on that side of his head was now nothing but a blackened lump.

Percy slapped the dead man's cheek. The flat smacking sound of his hand made us all jump. Percy looked around at us with a cocky smile on his mouth, eyes glittering. Then he looked back at Bitterbuck again. "Adiós, Chief," he said. "Hope hell's hot enough for you."

"Don't do that," Brutal said, his voice hollow and declamatory in the dripping tunnel. "He's paid what he owed. He's square with the house again. You keep your hands off him."

"Aw, blow it out," Percy said, but he stepped back uneasily when Brutal moved toward him, shadow rising behind him like the shadow of that ape in the story about the Rue Morgue. But instead of grabbing at Percy, Brutal grabbed hold of the gurney and began pushing Arlen Bitterbuck slowly toward the far end of the tunnel, where his last ride was waiting, parked on the soft shoulder of the highway. The gurney's hard rubber wheels moaned on the boards; its shadow rode the bulging brick wall, waxing and waning; Dean and Harry grasped the sheet at the foot and pulled it up over The Chief's face, which had already begun to take on the waxy, characterless cast of all dead faces, the innocent as well as the guilty.

6

When I was eighteen, my Uncle Paul—the man I was named for—died of a heart attack. My mother and dad took me to Chicago with them to attend his funeral and visit relatives from my father's side of the family, many of whom I had never met. We were gone almost a month. In some ways that was a good trip, a necessary and exciting trip, but in another way it was horrible. I was deeply in love, you see, with the young woman who was to become my wife two weeks after my nineteenth birthday. One night when my longing for her was like a fire burning out of control in my heart and my head (oh yes, all right, and in my balls, as well), I wrote her a letter that just seemed to go on and on—I poured out my whole heart in it, never looking back to see what I'd said because I was afraid cowardice would make me stop. I didn't stop, and when a voice in my head clamored that it would be madness to mail such a letter, that I would be giving her my naked heart to hold in her hand, I ignored it with a child's breathless disregard of the consequences. I often wondered if Janice kept that letter, but never quite got up enough courage to ask. All I know for sure is that I did not find it when I went through her things after the funeral, and of course that by itself means nothing. I suppose I never asked because I was afraid of discovering that burning epistle meant less to her than it did to me.

It was four pages long, I thought I would never write anything longer in my life, and now look at this. All this, and the end still not in sight. If I'd known the story was going to go on this long, I might never have started. What I didn't realize was how many doors the act of writing unlocks, as if my Dad's old fountain pen wasn't really a pen at all, but some strange variety of skeleton key. The mouse is probably the best example of what I'm talking about—Steamboat Willy, Mr. Jingles, the mouse on the Mile. Until I started to write, I never realized how important he (yes, *he*) was. The way he seemed to be looking for Delacroix before Delacroix arrived, for instance—I don't think that ever occurred to me, not to my conscious mind, anyway, until I began to write and remember.

I guess what I'm saying is that I didn't realize how far back I'd have to go in order to tell you about John Coffey, or how long I'd have to leave him there in his cell, a man so huge his feet didn't just stick off the end of his bunk but hung down all the way to the floor. I don't want you to forget him, all right? I want

you to see him there, looking up at the ceiling of his
cell, weeping his silent tears, or putting his arms over
his face. I want you to hear him, his sighs that trembled like sobs, his occasional watery groan. These
weren't the sounds of agony and regret we sometimes heard on E Block, sharp cries with splinters of
remorse in them; like his wet eyes, they were somehow removed from the pain we were used to dealing
with. In a way—I know how crazy this will sound, of
course I do, but there is no sense in writing something as long as this if you can't say what feels true
to your heart—in a way it was as if it was sorrow for
the whole world he felt, something too big ever to be
completely eased. Sometimes I sat and talked to him,
as I did with all of them—talking was our biggest,
most important job, as I believe I have said—and I
tried to comfort him. I don't feel that I ever did, and
part of my heart was glad he was suffering, you
know. Felt he *deserved* to suffer. I even thought sometimes of calling the governor (or getting Percy to do
it—hell, he was Percy's damn uncle, not mine) and
asking for a stay of execution. *We shouldn't burn him
yet*, I'd say. *It's still hurting him too much, biting into
him too much, twisting in his guts like a nice sharp stick.
Give him another ninety days, your honor, sir. Let him go
on doing to himself what we can't do to him.*

It's that John Coffey I'd have you keep to one side
of your mind while I finish catching up to where I
started—that John Coffey lying on his bunk, that
John Coffey who was afraid of the dark perhaps with

good reason, for in the dark might not two shapes with blonde curls—no longer little girls but avenging harpies—be waiting for him? That John Coffey whose eyes were always streaming tears, like blood from a wound that can never heal.

7

So The Chief burned and The President walked—
as far as C Block, anyway, which was home to
most of Cold Mountain's hundred and fifty lifers.
Life for The Pres turned out to be twelve years. He
was drowned in the prison laundry in 1944. Not the
Cold Mountain prison laundry; Cold Mountain
closed in 1933. I don't suppose it mattered much to
the inmates—walls is walls, as the cons say, and Old
Sparky was every bit as lethal in his own little stone
death chamber, I reckon, as he'd ever been in the
storage room at Cold Mountain.

As for The Pres, someone shoved him face-first
into a vat of dry-cleaning fluid and held him there.
When the guards pulled him out again, his face was
almost entirely gone. They had to ID him by his fin-
gerprints. On the whole, he might have been better
off with Old Sparky ... but then he never would
have had those extra twelve years, would he? I doubt
he thought much about them, though, in the last

minute or so of his life, when his lungs were trying to learn how to breathe Hexlite and lye cleanser.

They never caught whoever did for him. By then I was out of the corrections line of work, but Harry Terwilliger wrote and told me. "He got commuted mostly because he was white," Harry wrote, "but he got it in the end, just the same. I just think of it as a long stay of execution that finally ran out."

There was a quiet time for us in E Block, once The Pres was gone. Harry and Dean were temporarily re-assigned, and it was just me, Brutal, and Percy on the Green Mile for a little bit. Which actually meant just me and Brutal, because Percy kept pretty much to himself. I tell you, that young man was a genius at finding things not to do. And every so often (but only when Percy wasn't around), the other guys would show up to have what Harry liked to call "a good gab." On many of these occasions the mouse would also show up. We'd feed him and he'd sit there eating, just as solemn as Solomon, watching us with his bright little oilspot eyes.

That was a good few weeks, calm and easy even with Percy's more than occasional carping. But all good things come to an end, and on a rainy Monday in late July—have I told you how rainy and dank that summer was?—I found myself sitting on the bunk of an open cell and waiting for Eduard Delacroix.

He came with an unexpected bang. The door leading into the exercise yard slammed open, letting in a flood of light, there was a confused rattle of chains, a frightened voice babbling away in a mixture of English and Cajun French (a patois the cons at Cold Mountain used to call *da bayou*), and Brutal hollering, "Hey! Quit it! For Chrissakes! Quit it, Percy!"

I had been half-dozing on what was to become Delacroix's bunk, but I was up in a hurry, my heart slugging away hard in my chest. Noise of that kind on E Block almost never happened until Percy came; he brought it along with him like a bad smell.

"Come on, you fuckin French-fried faggot!" Percy yelled, ignoring Brutal completely. And here he came, dragging a guy not much bigger than a bowling pin by one arm. In his other hand, Percy had his baton. His teeth were bared in a strained grimace, and his face was bright red. Yet he did not look entirely unhappy. Delacroix was trying to keep up with him, but he had the legirons on, and no matter how fast he shuffled his feet, Percy pulled him along faster. I sprang out of the cell just in time to catch him as he fell, and that was how Del and I were introduced.

Percy rounded on him, baton raised, and I held him back with one arm. Brutal came puffing up to us, looking as shocked and nonplussed by all this as I felt.

"Don't let him hit me no mo, *m'sieu*," Delacroix babbled. "*S'il vous plaît, s'il vous plaît!*"

"Let me at im, let me at im!" Percy cried, lunging forward. He began to hit at Delacroix's shoulders with his baton. Delacroix held his arms up, scream-ing, and the stick went whap-whap-whap against the sleeves of his blue prison shirt. I saw him that night with the shirt off, and that boy had bruises from Christmas to Easter. Seeing them made me feel bad. He was a murderer, and nobody's darling, but that's not the way we did things on E Block. Not until Percy came, anyhow.

"Whoa! Whoa!" I roared. "Quit that! What's it all about, anyway?" I was trying to get my body in be-tween Delacroix's and Percy's, but it wasn't working very well. Percy's club continued to flail away, now on one side of me and now on the other. Sooner or later he was going to bring one down on *me* instead of on his intended target, and then there was going to be a brawl right here in this corridor, no matter who his relations were. I wouldn't be able to help myself, and Brutal was apt to join in. In some ways, you know, I wish we'd done it. It might have changed some of the things that happened later on.

"Fucking faggot! I'll teach you to keep your hands off me, you lousy bum-puncher!"

Whap! Whap! Whap! And now Delacroix was bleeding from one ear and screaming. I gave up try-ing to shield him, grabbed him by one shoulder, and hurled him into his cell, where he went sprawling on the bunk. Percy darted around me and gave him a fi-nal hard whap on the butt—one to go on, you could say. Then Brutal grabbed him—Percy, I mean—by the shoulders and hauled him across the corridor.

I grabbed the cell door and ran it shut on its tracks. Then I turned to Percy, my shock and bewilderment at war with pure fury. Percy had been around about several months at that point, long enough for all of us to decide we didn't like him very much, but that was the first time I fully understood how out of control he was.

He stood watching me, not entirely without fear—he was a coward at heart, I never had any doubt of that—but still confident that his connections would protect him. In that he was correct. I suspect there are people who wouldn't understand why that was, even after all I've said, but they would be people who only know the phrase *Great Depression* from the history books. If you were there, it was a lot more than a phrase in a book, and if you had a steady job, brother, you'd do almost anything to keep it.

The color was fading out of Percy's face a little by then, but his cheeks were still flushed, and his hair, which was usually swept back and gleaming with brilliantine, had tumbled over his forehead.

"What in the Christ was *that* all about?" I asked. "I have never—I have *never!*—had a prisoner beaten onto my block before!"

"Little fag bastard tried to cop my joint when I pulled him out of the van," Percy said. "He had it coming, and I'd do it again."

I looked at him, too flabbergasted for words. I couldn't imagine the most predatory homosexual on God's green earth doing what Percy had just described. Preparing to move into a crossbar apartment on the Green Mile did not, as a rule, put even the most deviant of prisoners in a sexy mood.

I looked back at Delacroix, cowering on his bunk with his arms still up to protect his face. There were cuffs on his wrists and a chain running between his ankles. Then I turned to Percy. "Get out of here," I said. "I'll want to talk to you later."

"Is this going to be in your report?" he demanded truculently. "Because if it is, I can make a report of my own, you know."

I didn't want to make a report; I only wanted him out of my sight. I told him so.

"The matter's closed," I finished. I saw Brutal looking at me disapprovingly, but ignored it. "Go on, get out of here. Go over to Admin and tell them you're supposed to read letters and help in the package room."

"Sure." He had his composure back, or the crackheaded arrogance that served him as composure. He brushed his hair back from his forehead with his hands—soft and white and small, the hands of a girl in her early teens, you would have thought—and then approached the cell. Delacroix saw him, and he cringed back even farther on his bunk, gibbering in a mixture of English and stewpot French.

"I ain't done with you, Pierre," he said, then jumped as one of Brutal's huge hands fell on his shoulder.

"Yes you are," Brutal said. "Now go on. Get in the breeze."

"You don't scare me, you know," Percy said. "Not a bit." His eyes shifted to me. "Either of you." But we did. You could see that in his eyes as clear as day, and it made him even more dangerous. A guy like Percy doesn't even know himself what he means to do from minute to minute and second to second.

What he did right then was turn away from us and go walking up the corridor in long, arrogant strides. He had shown the world what happened when scrawny, half-bald little Frenchmen tried to cop his joint, by God, and he was leaving the field a victor.

I went through my set speech, all about how we had the radio—*Make Believe Ballroom* and *Our Gal Sunday*, and how we'd treat him jake if he did the same for us. That little homily was not what you'd call one of my great successes. He cried all the way through it, sitting huddled up at the foot of his bunk, as far from me as he could get without actually fading into the corner. He cringed every time I moved, and I don't think he heard one word in six. Probably just as well. I don't think that particular homily made a whole lot of sense, anyway.

Fifteen minutes later I was back at the desk, where a shaken-looking Brutus Howell was sitting and licking the tip of the pencil we kept with the visitors' book. "Will you stop that before you poison yourself, for God's sake?" I asked.

"Christ almighty Jesus," he said, putting the pencil

down. "I *never* want to have another hooraw like that with a prisoner coming on the block."

"My Daddy always used to say things come in threes," I said.

"Well, I hope your Daddy was full of shit on that subject," Brutal said, but of course he wasn't. There was a squall when John Coffey came in, and a full-blown storm when "Wild Bill" joined us—it's funny, but things really *do* seem to come in threes. The story of our introduction to Wild Bill, how he came onto the Mile trying to commit murder, is something I'll get to shortly; fair warning.

"What's this about Delacroix copping his joint?" I asked.

Brutal snorted. "He was ankle-chained and ole Percy was just pulling him too fast, that's all. He stumbled and started to fall as he got out of the stagecoach. He put his hands out same as anyone would when they start to fall, and one of them brushed the front of Percy's pants. It was a complete accident."

"Did Percy know that, do you think?" I asked. "Was he maybe using it as an excuse just because he felt like whaling on Delacroix a little bit? Showing him who bosses the shooting match around here?"

Brutal nodded slowly. "Yeah. I think that was probably it."

"We have to watch him, then," I said, and ran my hands through my hair. As if the job wasn't hard enough. "God, I hate this. I hate *him*."

"Me, too. And you want to know something else, Paul? I don't understand him. He's got connections, I understand *that*, all right, but why would he use them to get a job on the Green fucking Mile? *Anywhere* in the state pen, for that matter? Why not as a page in the state senate, or the guy who makes the lieutenant governor's appointments? Surely his people could've gotten him something better if he'd asked them, so why *here*?"

I shook my head. I didn't know. There were a lot of things I didn't know then. I suppose I was naive.

8

After that, things went back to normal again . . . for awhile, at least. Down in the county seat, the state was preparing to bring John Coffey to trial, and Trapingus County Sheriff Homer Cribus was pooh-poohing the idea that a lynch-mob might hurry justice along a little bit. None of that mattered to us; on E Block, no one paid much attention to the news. Life on the Green Mile was, in a way, like life in a soundproof room. From time to time you heard mutterings that were probably explosions in the outside world, but that was about all. They wouldn't hurry with John Coffey; they'd want to make damned sure of him.

On a couple of occasions Percy got to ragging Delacroix, and the second time I pulled him aside and told him to come up to my office. It wasn't my first interview with Percy on the subject of his behavior, and it wouldn't be the last, but it was prompted by what was probably the clearest understanding of what he was. He had the heart of a cruel boy who goes to the zoo not so he can study the animals but so he can throw stones at them in their cages.

"You stay away from him, now, you hear?" I said. "Unless I give you a specific order, just stay the hell away from him."

Percy combed his hair back, then patted at it with his sweet little hands. That boy just loved touching his hair. "I wasn't doing nothing to him," he said. "Only asking how it felt to know you had burned up some babies, is all." Percy gave me a round-eyed, innocent stare.

"You quit with it, or there'll be a report," I said.

He laughed. "Make any report you want," he said. "Then I'll turn around and make my own. Just like I told you when he came in. We'll see who comes off the best."

I leaned forward, hands folded on my desk, and spoke in a tone I hoped would sound like a friend being confidential. "Brutus Howell doesn't like you much," I said. "And when Brutal doesn't like someone, he's been known to make his own report. He isn't much shakes with a pen, and he can't quit from licking that pencil, so he's apt to report with his fists. If you know what I mean."

Percy's complacent little smile faltered. "What are you trying to say"

"I'm not *trying* to say anything. I *have* said it. And if you tell any of your ... friends ... about this discussion, I'll say you made the whole thing up." I looked at him all wide-eyed and earnest. "Besides,

I'm trying to be your friend, Percy. A word to the wise is sufficient, they say. And why would you want to get into it with Delacroix in the first place? He's not worth it."

And for awhile that worked. There was peace. A couple of times I was even able to send Percy with Dean or Harry when Delacroix's time to shower had rolled around. We had the radio at night, Delacroix began to relax a little into the scant routine of E Block, and there was peace.

Then, one night, I heard him laughing.

Harry Terwilliger was on the desk, and soon he was laughing, too. I got up and went on down to Delacroix's cell to see what he possibly had to laugh about.

"Look, Cap'n!" he said when he saw me. "I done tame me a mouse!"

It was Steamboat Willy. He was in Delacroix's cell. More: he was sitting on Delacroix's shoulder and looking calmly out through the bars at us with his little oildrop eyes. His tail was curled around his paws, and he looked completely at peace. As for Delacroix—friend, you wouldn't have known it was the same man who'd sat cringing and shuddering at the foot of his bunk not a week before. He looked like my daughter used to on Christmas morning, when she came down the stairs and saw the presents.

"Watch dis!" Delacroix said. The mouse was sitting on his right shoulder. Delacroix stretched out his left arm. The mouse scampered up to the top of Delacroix's head, using the man's hair (which was thick enough in back, at least) to climb up. Then he scampered down the other side, Delacroix giggling as his tail tickled the side of his neck. The mouse ran all the way down his arm to his wrist, then turned, scampered back up to Delacroix's left shoulder, and curled his tail around his feet again.

"I'll be damned," Harry said.

"I train him to do that," Delacroix said proudly. I thought, *In a pig's ass you did*, but kept my mouth shut. "His name is Mr. Jingles."

"Nah," Harry said goodnaturedly. "It's Steamboat Willy, like in the pitcher-show. Boss Howell named him."

"It's Mr. Jingles," Delacroix said. On any other subject he would have told you that shit was Shinola, if you wanted him to, but on the subject of the mouse's name he was perfectly adamant. "He whisper it in my ear. Cap'n, can I have a box for him? Can I have a box for my mous', so he can sleep in here wit me?" His voice began to fall into wheedling tones I had heard a thousand times before. "I put him under my bunk and he never be a scrid of trouble, not one."

"Your English gets a hell of a lot better when you want something," I said, stalling for time.

"Oh-oh," Harry murmured, nudging me. "Here comes trouble."

But Percy didn't look like trouble to me, not that night. He wasn't running his hands through his hair or fiddling with that baton of his, and the top button of his uniform shirt was actually undone. It was the first time I'd seen him that way, and it was amazing, what a change a little thing like that could make. Mostly, though, what struck me was the expression on his face. There was a calmness there. Not serenity—I don't think Percy Wetmore had a serene bone in his body—but the look of a man who has discovered he can wait for the things he wants. It was quite a change from the young man I'd had to threaten with Brutus Howell's fists only a few days before.

Delacroix didn't see the change, though; he cringed against the wall of his cell, drawing his knees up to his chest. His eyes seemed to grow until they were taking up half his face. The mouse scampered up on his bald pate and sat there. I don't know if he remembered that he also had reason to distrust Percy, but it certainly looked as if he did. Probably it was just smelling the little Frenchman's fear, and reacting off that.

"Well, well," Percy said. "Looks like you found yourself a friend, Eddie."

Delacroix tried to reply—some hollow defiance about what would happen to Percy if Percy hurt his new pal would have been my guess—but nothing came out. His lower lip trembled a little, but that was all. On top of his head, Mr. Jingles wasn't trembling. He sat perfectly still with his back feet in Delacroix's hair and his front ones splayed on Delacroix's bald skull, looking at Percy, seeming to size him up. The way you'd size up an old enemy.

Percy looked at me. "Isn't that the same one I chased? The one that lives in the restraint room?"

I nodded. I had an idea Percy hadn't seen the newly named Mr. Jingles since that last chase, and he showed no signs of wanting to chase it now.

"Yes, that's the one," I said. "Only Delacroix there says his name is Mr. Jingles, not Steamboat Willy. Says the mouse whispered it in his ear."

"Is that so," Percy said. "Wonders never cease, do they?" I half-expected him to pull out his baton and start tapping it against the bars, just to show Delacroix who was boss, but he only stood there with his hands on his hips, looking in.

And for no reason I could have told you in words, I said: "Delacroix there was just asking for a box, Percy. He thinks that mouse will sleep in it, I guess. That he can keep it for a pet." I loaded my voice with skepticism, and sensed more than saw Harry looking at me in surprise. "What do you think about that?"

"I think it'll probably shit up his nose some night while he's sleeping and then run away," Percy said evenly, "but I guess that's the French boy's lookout. I seen a pretty nice cigar box on Toot-Toot's cart the other night. I don't know if he'd give it away, though. Probably want a nickel for it, maybe even a dime."

Now I did risk a glance at Harry, and saw his mouth hanging open. This wasn't quite like the change in Ebenezer Scrooge on Christmas morning, after the ghosts had had their way with him, but it was damned close.

Percy leaned closer to Delacroix, putting his face between the bars. Delacroix shrank back even farther. I swear to God that he would have melted into that wall if he'd been able.

"You got a nickel or maybe as much as a dime to pay for a cigar box, you lugoon?" he asked.

"I got four pennies," Delacroix said. "I give them for a box, if it a good one, *s'il est bon.*"

"I'll tell you what," Percy said. "If that toothless old whoremaster will sell you that Corona box for four cents, I'll sneak some cotton batting out of the dispensary to line it with. We'll make us a regular Mousie Hilton, before we're through." He shifted his eyes to me. "I'm supposed to write a switch-room report about Bitterbuck," he said. "Is there some pens in your office, Paul?"

"Yes, indeed," I said. "Forms, too. Lefthand top drawer."

"Well, that's aces," he said, and went swaggering off.

Harry and I looked at each other. "Is he sick, do you think?" Harry asked. "Maybe went to his doctor and found out he's only got three months to live?"

I told him I didn't have the slightest idea what was up. It was the truth then, and for awhile after, but I found out in time. And a few years later, I had an interesting supper-table conversation with Hal Moores. By then we could talk freely, what with him being retired and me being at the Boys' Correctional. It was one of those meals where you drink too much and eat too little, and tongues get loosened. Hal told me that Percy had been in to complain about me and about life on the Mile in general. This was just after Delacroix came on the block, and Brutal and I had kept Percy from beating him half to death. What had griped Percy the most was me telling him to get out of my sight. He didn't think a man who was related to the governor should have to put up with talk like that.

Well, Moores told me, he had stood Percy off for as long as he could, and when it became clear to him that Percy was going to try pulling some strings to get me reprimanded and moved to another part of the prison at the very least, he, Moores, had pulled Percy into his office and told him that if he quit rocking the boat, Moores would make sure that Percy was out front for Delacroix's execution. That he would, in fact, be placed right beside the chair. I would be in charge, as always, but the witnesses wouldn't know that; to them it would look as if Mr. Percy Wetmore was boss of the cotillion. Moores wasn't promising any more than what we'd already discussed and I'd gone along with, but Percy didn't know that. He agreed to leave off his threats to have me reassigned, and the atmosphere on E Block sweetened. He had even agreed that Delacroix could keep Percy's old nemesis as a pet. It's amazing how some men can change, given the right incentive; in Percy's case, all Warden Moores had to offer was the chance to take a bald little Frenchman's life.

9

Toot-Toot felt that four cents was far too little for a prime Corona cigar box, and in that he was probably right—cigar boxes were highly prized objects in prison. A thousand different small items could be stored in them, the smell was pleasant, and there was something about them that reminded our customers of what it was like to be free men. Because cigarettes were permitted in prison but cigars were not, I imagine.

Dean Stanton, who was back on the block by then, added a penny to the pot, and I kicked one in, as well. When Toot still proved reluctant, Brutal went to work on him, first telling him he ought to be ashamed of himself for behaving like such a cheapskate, then promising him that he, Brutus Howell, would personally put that Corona box back in Toot's hands the day after Delacroix's execution. "Six cents might or might not be enough if you was speaking about *selling* that cigar box, we could have a good old barber-shop argument about that," Brutal said, "but you have to admit it's a great price for *renting* one. He's gonna walk the Mile in a month, six weeks at the very outside. Why, that box'll be back on the shelf under your cart almost before you know it's gone."

"He could get a soft-hearted judge to give im a stay and still be here to sing 'Should old acquaintances be forgot,' " Toot said, but he knew better and Brutal knew he did. Old Toot-Toot had been pushing that damned Bible-quoting cart of his around Cold Mountain since Pony Express days, practically, and he had plenty of sources . . . better than ours, I thought then. He knew Delacroix was fresh out of soft-hearted judges. All he had left to hope for was the governor, who as a rule didn't issue clemency to folks who had baked half a dozen of his constituents.

"Even if he don't get a stay, that mouse'd be shitting in that box until October, maybe even Thanksgiving," Toot argued, but Brutal could see he was weakening. "Who gonna buy a cigar box some mouse been using for a toilet?"

"Oh jeez-Louise," Brutal said. "That's the numbest thing I've ever heard you say, Toot. I mean, that takes the cake. First, Delacroix will keep the box clean enough to eat a church dinner out of—the way he loves that mouse, he'd lick it clean if that's what it took."

"Easy on dat stuff," Toot said, wrinkling his nose.

"Second," Brutal went on, "mouse-shit is no big deal, anyway. It's just hard little pellets, looks like birdshot. Shake it right out. Nothing to it."

Old Toot knew better than to carry his protest any further; he'd been on the yard long enough to understand when he could afford to face into the breeze and when he'd do better to bend in the hurricane. This wasn't exactly a hurricane, but we bluesuits liked the mouse, and we liked the idea of Delacroix having the mouse, and that meant it was at least a gale. So Delacroix got his box, and Percy was as good as his word—two days later the bottom was lined with soft pads of cotton batting from the dispensary. Percy handed them over himself, and I could see the fear in Delacroix's eyes as he reached out through the bars to take them. He was afraid Percy would grab his hand and break his fingers. I was a little afraid of it, too, but no such thing happened. That was the closest I ever came to liking Percy, but even then it was hard to mistake the look of cool amusement in his eyes. Delacroix had a pet; Percy had one, too. Delacroix would keep his, petting it and loving it as long as he could; Percy would wait patiently (as patiently as a man like him could, anyway), and then burn his alive.

"Mousie Hilton, open for business," Harry said. "The only question is, will the little bugger use it?"

That question was answered as soon as Delacroix caught Mr. Jingles up in one hand and lowered him gently into the box. The mouse snuggled into the white cotton as if it were Aunt Bea's comforter, and that was his home from then until . . . well, I'll get to the end of Mr. Jingles's story in good time.

Old Toot-Toot's worries that the cigar box would
fill up with mouse-shit proved to be entirely ground-
less. I never saw a single turd in there, and Delacroix
said he never did, either . . . anywhere in his cell, for
that matter. Much later, around the time Brutal
showed me the hole in the beam and we found the
colored splinters, I moved a chair out of the restraint
room's east corner and found a little pile of mouse
turds back there. He had always gone back to the
same place to do his business, seemingly, and as far
from us as he could get. Here's another thing: I never
saw him peeing, and usually mice can hardly turn
the faucet off for two minutes at a time, especially
while they're eating. I told you, the damned thing
was one of God's mysteries.

A week or so after Mr. Jingles had settled into the
cigar box, Delacroix called me and Brutal down to
his cell to see something. He did that so much it was
annoying—if Mr. Jingles so much as rolled over on
his back with his paws in the air, it was the cutest
thing on God's earth, as far as that half-pint Cajun
was concerned—but this time what he was up to really was sort of amusing.

Delacroix had been pretty much forgotten by the
world following his conviction, but he had one rela-
tion—an old maiden aunt, I believe—who wrote him
once a week. She had also sent him an enormous bag
of peppermint candies, the sort which are marketed
under the name Canada Mints these days. They
looked like big pink pills. Delacroix was not allowed

to have the whole bag at once, naturally—it was a five-pounder, and he would have gobbled them until he had to go to the infirmary with stomach-gripes. Like almost every murderer we ever had on the Mile, he had absolutely no understanding of moderation. We'd give them out to him half a dozen at a time, and only then if he remembered to ask.

Mr. Jingles was sitting beside Delacroix on the bunk when we got down there, holding one of those pink candies in his paws and munching contentedly away at it. Delacroix was simply overcome with delight—he was like a classical pianist watching his five-year-old son play his first halting exercises. But don't get me wrong; it *was* funny, a real hoot. The candy was half the size of Mr. Jingles, and his white-furred belly was already distended from it.

"Take it away from him, Eddie," Brutal said, half-laughing and half-horrified. "Christ almighty Jesus, he'll eat till he busts. I can smell that peppermint from here. How many have you let him have?"

"This his second," Delacroix said, looking a little nervously at Mr. Jingles's belly. "You really think he . . . you know . . . bus' his guts?"

"Might," Brutal said.

That was enough authority for Delacroix. He reached for the half-eaten pink mint. I expected the mouse to nip him, but Mr. Jingles gave over that mint—what remained of it, anyway—as meek as could be. I looked at Brutal, and Brutal gave his head a little shake as if to say no, he didn't understand it, either. Then Mr. Jingles plopped down into his box and lay there on his side in an exhausted way that made all three of us laugh. After that, we got used to seeing the mouse sitting beside Delacroix, holding a mint and munching away on it just as neatly as an old lady at an afternoon tea-party, both of them sur-rounded by what I later smelled in that hole in the beam—the half-bitter, half-sweet smell of peppermint candy.

There's one more thing to tell you about Mr. Jin-gles before moving on to the arrival of William Wharton, which was when the cyclone really touched down on E Block. A week or so after the incident of the peppermint candies—around the time when we'd pretty much decided Delacroix wasn't going to feed his pet to death, in other words—the Frenchman called me down to his cell. I was on my own for the time being, Brutal over at the commissary for some-thing, and according to the regs, I was not supposed to approach a prisoner in such circumstances. But since I probably could have shot-putted Delacroix twenty yards one-handed on a good day, I decided to break the rule and see what he wanted.

"Watch this, Boss Edgecombe," he said. "You gonna see what Mr. Jingles can do!" He reached be-hind the cigar box and brought up a small wooden spool.

"Where'd you get that?" I asked him, although I supposed I knew. There was really only one person he *could* have gotten it from.

"Old Toot-Toot," he said. "Watch this."

I was already watching, and could see Mr. Jingles in his box, standing up with his small front paws propped on the edge, his black eyes fixed on the spool Delacroix was holding between the thumb and first finger of his right hand. I felt a funny little chill go up my back. I had never seen a mere mouse attend to something with such sharpness—with such *intelligence*. I don't really believe that Mr. Jingles was a supernatural visitation, and if I have given you that idea, I'm sorry, but I have never doubted that he was a genius of his kind.

Delacroix bent over and rolled the threadless spool across the floor of his cell. It went easily, like a pair of wheels connected by an axle. The mouse was out of his box in a flash and across the floor after it, like a dog chasing after a stick. I exclaimed with surprise, and Delacroix grinned.

The spool hit the wall and rebounded. Mr. Jingles went around it and pushed it back to the bunk, switching from one end of the spool to the other whenever it looked like it was going to veer off-course. He pushed the spool until it hit Delacroix's foot. Then he looked up at him for a moment, as if to make sure Delacroix had no more immediate tasks for him (a few arithmetic problems to solve, perhaps, or some Latin to parse). Apparently satisfied on this score, Mr. Jingles went back to the cigar box and settled down in it again.

"You taught him that," I said.

"Yessir, Boss Edgecombe," Delacroix said, his smile only slightly dissembling. "He fetch it every time. Smart as hell, ain't he?"

"And the spool?" I asked. "How did you know to fetch that for *him*, Eddie?"

"He whisper in my ear that he want it," Delacroix said serenely. "Same as he whisper his name."

Delacroix showed all the other guys his mouse's trick . . . all except Percy. To Delacroix, it didn't matter that Percy had suggested the cigar box and procured the cotton with which to line it. Delacroix was like some dogs: kick them once and they never trust you again, no matter how nice you are to them.

I can hear Delacroix now, yelling, *Hey, you guys! Come and see what Mr. Jingles can do!* And them going down in a bluesuit cluster—Brutal, Harry, Dean, even Bill Dodge. All of them had been properly amazed, too, the same as I had been.

Three or four days after Mr. Jingles started doing the trick with the spool, Harry Terwilliger rummaged through the arts and crafts stuff we kept in the restraint room, found the Crayolas, and brought them to Delacroix with a smile that was almost embarrassed. "I thought you might like to make that spool different colors," he said. "Then your little pal'd be like a circus mouse, or something."

"A circus mouse!" Delacroix said, looking completely, rapturously happy. I suppose he *was* completely happy, maybe for the first time in his whole miserable life. "That just what he is, too! A circus mouse! When I get outta here, he gonna make me rich, like inna circus! You see if he don't."

Percy Wetmore would no doubt have pointed out to Delacroix that when he left Cold Mountain, he'd be riding in an ambulance that didn't need to run its light or siren, but Harry knew better. He just told Delacroix to make the spool as colorful as he could as quick as he could, because he'd have to take the crayons back after dinner.

Del made it colorful, all right. When he was done, one end of the spool was yellow, the other end was green, and the drum in the middle was firehouse red. We got used to hearing Delacroix trumpet, *"Maintenant, m'sieurs et mesdames! Le cirque présentement le mous' amusant et amazeant!"* That wasn't exactly it, but it gives you an idea of that stewpot French of his. Then he'd make this sound way down in his throat—I think it was supposed to represent a drumroll—and fling the spool. Mr. Jingles would be after it in a flash, either nosing it back or rolling it with his paws. That second way really was something you would have paid to see in a circus, I think. Delacroix and his mouse and his mouse's brightly colored spool were our chief amusements at the time that John Coffey came into our care and custody, and that was the way things remained for awhile. Then my urinary infection, which had lain still for awhile, came back, and William Wharton arrived, and all hell broke loose.

10

The dates have mostly slipped out of my head. I suppose I could have my granddaughter, Danielle, look some of them out of the old newspaper files, but what would be the point? The most important of them, like the day we came down to Delacroix's cell and found the mouse sitting on his shoulder, or the day William Wharton came on the block and almost killed Dean Stanton, would not be in the papers, anyway. Maybe it's better to go on just as I have been; in the end, I guess the dates don't matter much, if you can remember the things you saw and keep them in the right order.

I know that things got squeezed together a little. When Delacroix's DOE papers finally came to me from Curtis Anderson's office, I was amazed to see that our Cajun pal's date with Old Sparky had been advanced from when we had expected, a thing that was almost unheard of, even in those days when you didn't have to move half of heaven and all the earth to execute a man. It was a matter of two days, I think, from the twenty-seventh of October to the twenty-fifth. Don't hold me to it exactly, but I know that's close; I remember thinking that Toot was going to get his Corona box back even sooner than he had expected.

Wharton, meanwhile, got to us later than expected. For one thing, his trial ran longer than Anderson's usually reliable sources had thought it would (when it came to Wild Billy, *nothing* was reliable, we would soon discover, including our time-tested and supposedly foolproof methods of prisoner control). Then, after he had been found guilty—that much, at least, went according to the script—he was taken to Indianola General Hospital for tests. He had had a number of supposed seizures during the trial, twice serious enough to send him crashing to the floor, where he lay shaking and flopping and drumming his feet on the boards. Wharton's court-appointed lawyer claimed he suffered from "epilepsy spells" and had committed his crimes while of unsound mind; the prosecution claimed the fits were the sham acting of a coward desperate to save his own life. After observing the so-called "epilepsy spells" at first hand, the jury decided the fits were an act. The judge concurred but ordered a series of pre-sentencing tests after the verdict came down. God knows why; perhaps he was only curious.

It's a blue-eyed wonder that Wharton didn't escape from the hospital (and the irony that Warden Moores's wife, Melinda, was in the same hospital at the same time did not escape any of us), but he didn't. They had him surrounded by guards, I suppose, and perhaps he still had hopes of being declared incompetent by reason of epilepsy, if there is such a thing.

He wasn't. The doctors found nothing wrong with his brain—physiologically, at least—and Billy "the Kid" Wharton was at last bound for Cold Mountain. That might have been around the sixteenth or the eighteenth; it's my recollection that Wharton arrived about two weeks after John Coffey and a week or ten days before Delacroix walked the Green Mile.

The day our new psychopath joined us was an eventful one for me. I woke up at four that morning with my groin throbbing and my penis feeling hot and clogged and swollen. Even before I swung my feet out of bed, I knew that my urinary infection wasn't getting better, as I had hoped. It had been a brief turn for the better, that was all, and it was over.

I went out to the privy to do my business—this was at least three years before we put in our first water-closet—and had gotten no further than the woodpile at the corner of the house when I realized I couldn't hold it any longer. I lowered my pajama pants just as the urine started to flow, and that flow was accompanied by the most excruciating pain of my entire life. I passed a gall-stone in 1956, and I know people say that is the worst, but that gall-stone was like a touch of acid indigestion compared to this outrage.

My knees came unhinged and I fell heavily onto them, tearing out the seat of my pajama pants when I spread my legs to keep from losing my balance and going face-first into a puddle of my own piss. I still might have gone over if I hadn't grabbed one of the woodpile logs with my left hand. All that, though, could have been going on in Australia, or even on another planet. All I was concerned with was the pain that had set me on fire; my lower belly was burning, and my penis—an organ which had gone mostly forgotten by me except when providing me the most intense physical pleasure a man can experience—now felt as if it were melting; I expected to look down and see blood gushing from its tip, but it appeared to be a perfectly ordinary stream of urine.

I hung onto the woodpile with one hand and put the other across my mouth, concentrating on keeping my mouth shut. I did not want to frighten my wife awake with a scream. It seemed that I went on pissing forever, but at last the stream dried up. By then the pain had sunk deep into my stomach and my testicles, biting like rusty teeth. For a long while—it might have been as long as a minute—I was physically incapable of getting up. At last the pain began to abate, and I struggled to my feet. I looked at my urine, already soaking into the ground, and wondered if any sane God could make a world where such a little bit of dampness could come at the cost of such horrendous pain.

I would call in sick, I thought, and go see Dr. Sadler after all. I didn't want the stink and the queasiness of Dr. Sadler's sulfa tablets, but anything would be better than kneeling beside the woodpile, trying not to scream while my prick was reporting that it had apparently been doused with coal-oil and set afire.

Then, as I was swallowing aspirin in our kitchen and listening to Jan snore lightly in the other room, I remembered that today was the day William Wharton was scheduled on the block, and that Brutal wouldn't be there—the roster had him over on the other side of the prison, helping to move the rest of the library and some leftover infirmary equipment to the new building. One thing I didn't feel right about in spite of my pain was leaving Wharton to Dean and Harry. They were good men, but Curtis Anderson's report had suggested that William Wharton was exceptionally bad news. This man just doesn't care, he had written, underlining for emphasis.

By then the pain had abated some, and I could think. The best idea, it seemed to me, was to leave for the prison early. I could get there at six, which was the time Warden Moores usually came in. He could get Brutus Howell reassigned to E Block long enough for Wharton's reception, and I'd make my long-overdue trip to the doctor. Cold Mountain was actually on my way.

Twice on the twenty-mile ride to the penitentiary,

that sudden need to urinate overcame me. Both times I was able to pull over and take care of the problem without embarrassing myself (for one thing, traffic on country roads at such an hour was all but nonexistent). Neither of these two voidings was as painful as the one that had taken me off my feet on the way to the privy, but both times I had to clutch the passenger-side doorhandle of my little Ford coupe to hold myself up, and I could feel sweat running down my hot face. I was sick, all right, good and sick.

I made it, though, drove in through the south gate, parked in my usual place, and went right up to see the warden. It was going on six o'clock by then. Miss Hannah's office was empty—she wouldn't be in until the relatively civilized hour of seven—but the light was on in Moores's office; I could see it through the pebbled glass. I gave a perfunctory knock and opened the door. Moores looked up, startled to see anyone at that unusual hour, and I would have given a great deal not to have been the one to see him in that condition, with his face naked and unguarded. His white hair, usually so neatly combed, was sticking up in tufts and tangles; his hands were in it, yanking and pulling, when I walked in. His eyes were raw, the skin beneath them puffy and swollen. His palsy was the worst I had ever seen it; he looked like a man who had just come inside after a long walk on a terribly cold night.

"Hal, I'm sorry, I'll come back—" I began.

"No," he said. "Please, Paul. Come in. Shut the

door and come in. I need someone now, if I ever needed anyone in my whole life. Shut the door and come in."

I did as he asked, forgetting my own pain for the first time since I'd awakened that morning.

"It's a brain tumor," Moores said. "They got X-ray pictures of it. They seemed real pleased with their pictures, actually. One of them said they may be the best ones anyone's ever gotten, at least so far; said they're going to publish them in some biggety medical journal up in New England. It's the size of a lemon, they said, and way down deep inside, where they can't operate. They say she'll be dead by Christmas. I haven't told her. I can't think how. I can't think how for the life of me."

Then he began to cry, big, gasping sobs that filled me with both pity and a kind of terror—when a man who keeps himself as tightly guarded as Hal Moores finally does lose control, it's frightening to watch. I stood there for a moment, then went to him and put my arm around his shoulders. He groped out for me with both of his own arms, like a drowning man, and began to sob against my stomach, all restraint washed away. Later, after he got himself under control, he apologized. He did it without quite meeting my eyes, as a man does when he feels he has embarrassed himself dreadfully, maybe so deeply that he can never quite live it down. A man can end up hating the fellow who has seen him in such a state. I thought Warden Moores was better than that, but it

never crossed my mind to do the business I had orig-
inally come for, and when I left Moores's office, I
walked over to E Block instead of back to my car.
The aspirin was working by then, and the pain in my
midsection was down to a low throb. I would get
through the day somehow, I reckoned, get Wharton
settled in, check back with Hal Moores that afternoon, and get my sick-leave for tomorrow. The worst
was pretty much over, I thought, with no slightest
idea that the worst of that day's mischief hadn't even
begun.

11

"We thought he was still doped from the tests," Dean said late that afternoon. His voice was low, rasping, almost a bark, and there were blackish-purple bruises rising on his neck. I could see it was hurting him to talk and thought of telling him to let it go, but sometimes it hurts more to be quiet. I judged that this was one of those times, and kept my own mouth shut. "We all thought he was doped, didn't we?"

Harry Terwilliger nodded. Even Percy, sitting off by himself in his own sullen little party of one, nodded.

Brutal glanced at me, and for a moment I met his eyes. We were thinking pretty much that same thing, that this was the way it happened. You were cruising along, everything going according to Hoyle, you made one mistake, and bang, the sky fell down on you. They had thought he was doped, it was a reasonable assumption to make, but no one had *asked* if he was doped. I thought I saw something else in Brutal's eyes, as well: Harry and Dean would learn from their mistake. Especially Dean, who could easily have gone home to his family dead. Percy wouldn't. Percy maybe couldn't. All Percy could do was sit in the corner and sulk because he was in the shit again.

There were seven of them that went up to Indianola to take charge of Wild Bill Wharton: Harry, Dean, Percy, two other guards in the back (I have forgotten their names, although I'm sure I knew them once), plus two up front. They took what we used to call the stagecoach—a Ford panel-truck which had been steel-reinforced and equipped with supposedly bulletproof glass. It looked like a cross between a milk-wagon and an armored car.

Harry Terwilliger was technically in charge of the expedition. He handed his paperwork over to the county sheriff (not Homer Cribus but some other elected yokel like him, I imagine), who in turn handed over Mr. William Wharton, hellraiser *extraordinaire*, as Delacroix might have put it. A Cold Mountain prison uniform had been sent ahead, but the sheriff and his men hadn't bothered to put Wharton in it; they left that to our boys. Wharton was dressed in a cotton hospital johnny and cheap felt slippers when they first met him on the second floor of the General Hospital, a scrawny man with a narrow, pimply face and a lot of long, tangly blond hair. His ass, also narrow and also covered with pimples, stuck out the back of the johnny. That was the part of him Harry and the others saw first, because Wharton was standing at the window and looking out at the parking lot when they came in. He didn't turn but just stood there, holding the curtains back with one hand, silent as a doll, while Harry bitched at the county sheriff about being too lazy to get Wharton into his prison blues and the county sheriff lectured—as every county official I've ever met seems bound to do—about what was his job and what was not.

When Harry got tired of that part (I doubt it took him long), he told Wharton to turn around. Wharton did. He looked, Dean told us in his raspy bark of a half-choked voice, like any one of a thousand back-country stampeders who had wound their way through Cold Mountain during our years there. Boil that look down and what you got was a dullard with a mean steak. Sometimes you also discovered a yellow streak in them, once their backs were to the wall, but more often there was nothing there but fight and mean and then more fight and more mean. There are people who see nobility in folks like Billy Wharton, but I am not one of them. A rat will fight, too, if it is cornered. This man's face seemed to have no more personality than his acne-studded backside, Dean told us. His jaw was slack, his eyes distant, his shoulders slumped, his hands dangling. He looked shot up with morphine, all right, every bit as coo-coo as any dopefiend any of them had ever seen.

At this, Percy gave another of his sullen nods.

"Put this on," Harry said, indicating the uniform on the foot of the bed—it had been taken out of the brown paper it was wrapped in, but otherwise not touched—it was still folded just as it had been in the prison laundry, with a pair of white cotton boxer shorts poking out of one shirtsleeve and a pair of white socks poking out of the other.

Wharton seemed willing enough to comply, but wasn't able to get very far without help. He managed the boxers, but when it came to the pants, he kept trying to put both legs into the same hole. Finally Dean helped him, getting his feet to go where they belonged and then yanking the trousers up, doing the fly, and snapping the waistband. Wharton only stood there, not even trying to help once he saw that Dean was doing it for him. He stared vacantly across the room, hands lax, and it didn't occur to any of them that he was shamming. Not in hopes of escape (at least I don't believe that was it) but only in hopes of making the maximum amount of trouble when the right time came.

The papers were signed. William Wharton, who had become county property when he was arrested, now became the state's property. He was taken down the back stairs and through the kitchen, surrounded by bluesuits. He walked with his head down and his long-fingered hands dangling. The first time his cap fell off, Dean put it back on him. The second time, he just tucked it into his own back pocket.

He had another chance to make trouble in the back of the stagecoach, when they were shackling him, and didn't. If he thought (even now I'm not sure if he did, or if he did, how much), he must have thought that the space was too small and the numbers too great to cause a satisfactory hooraw. So on went the chains, one set running between his ankles and another set— too long, it turned out—between his wrists.

The drive to Cold Mountain took an hour. During that whole time, Wharton sat on the lefthand bench up by the cab, head lowered, cuffed hands dangling between his knees. Every now and then he hummed a little, Harry said, and Percy roused himself enough from his funk to say that the lugoon dripped spittle from his lax lower lip, a drop at a time, until it had made a puddle between his feet. Like a dog dripping off the end of its tongue on a hot summer day.

They drove in through the south gate when they got to the pen, right past my car, I guess. The guard on the south pass ran back the big door between the lot and the exercise yard, and the stagecoach drove through. It was a slack time in the yard, not many men out and most of them hoeing in the garden. Pumpkin time, it would have been. They drove straight across to E Block and stopped. The driver opened the door and told them he was going to take the stagecoach over to the motor-pool to have the oil changed, it had been good working with them. The extra guards went with the vehicle, two of them sitting in the back eating apples, the doors now swinging open.

That left Dean, Harry, and Percy with one shackled prisoner. It should have been enough, *would* have been enough, if they hadn't been lulled by the stick-thin country boy standing head-down there in the dirt with chains on his wrists and ankles. They marched him the twelve or so paces to the door that opened into E Block, falling into the same formation we used when escorting prisoners down the Green Mile. Harry was on his left, Dean was on his right, and Percy was behind, with his baton in his hand. No one told me that, but I know damned well he had it out; Percy loved that hickory stick. As for me, I was sitting in what would be Wharton's home until it came time for him to check into the hot place—first cell on the right as you headed down the corridor toward the restraint room. I had my clipboard in my hands and was thinking of nothing but making my little set speech and getting the hell out. The pain in my groin was building up again, and all I wanted was to go into my office and wait for it to pass.

Dean stepped forward to unlock the door. He selected the right key from the bunch on his belt and slid it into the lock. Wharton came alive just as Dean turned the key and pulled the handle. He voiced a screaming, gibbering cry—a kind of Rebel yell—that froze Harry to temporary immobility and pretty much finished Percy Wetmore for the entire encounter. I heard that scream through the partly opened door and didn't associate it with anything human at first; I thought a dog had gotten into the yard somehow and had been hurt; that perhaps some mean-tempered con had hit it with a hoe.

Wharton lifted his arms, dropped the chain which

hung between his wrists over Dean's head, and commenced to choke him with it. Dean gave a strangled cry and lurched forward, into the cool electric light of our little world. Wharton was happy to go with him, even gave him a shove, all the time yelling and gibbering, even laughing. He had his arms cocked at the elbows with his fists up by Dean's ears, yanking the chain as tight as he could, whipsawing it back and forth.

Harry landed on Wharton's back, wrapping one hand in our new boy's greasy blond hair and slamming his other fist into the side of Wharton's face as hard as he could. He had both a baton of his own and a sidearm pistol, but in his excitement drew neither. We'd had trouble with prisoners before, you bet, but never one who'd taken any of us by surprise the way that Wharton did. The man's slyness was beyond our experience. I had never seen its like before, and have never seen it again.

And he was strong. All that slack looseness was gone. Harry said later that it was like jumping onto a coiled nest of steel springs that had somehow come to life. Wharton, now inside and near the duty desk, whirled to his left and flung Harry off. Harry hit the desk and went sprawling.

"Whoooee, boys!" Wharton laughed. "Ain't this a party, now? Is it, or what?"

Still screaming and laughing, Wharton went back to choking Dean with his chain. Why not? Wharton knew what we all knew: they could only fry him once.

"Hit him, Percy, hit him!" Harry screamed, struggling to his feet. But Percy only stood there, hickory baton in hand, eyes as wide as soup-plates. Here was the chance he'd been looking for, you would have said, his golden opportunity to put that tallywhacker of his to good use, and he was too scared and confused to do it. This wasn't some terrified little Frenchman or a black giant who hardly seemed to be in his own body; this was a whirling devil.

I came out of Wharton's cell, dropping my clipboard and pulling my .38. I had forgotten the infection that was heating up my middle for the second time that day. I didn't doubt the story the others told of Wharton's blank face and dull eyes when they told it, but that wasn't the Wharton I saw. What I saw was the face of an animal—not an intelligent animal, but one filled with cunning . . . and meanness . . . and joy. Yes. He was doing what he had been made to do. The place and the circumstances didn't matter. The other thing I saw was Dean Stanton's red, swelling face. He was dying in front of my eyes. Wharton saw the gun and turned Dean toward it, so that I'd almost certainly have to hit one to hit the other. From over Dean's shoulder, one blazing blue eye dared me to shoot.

To Be Continued

THE GREAT ESCAPE

Stay tuned to *The Green Mile* serial thriller for your chance to WIN over 1,000 AIR MILES awards in each episode up to Part 5, with a massive 6,000 AIR MILES awards to be won in Part 6 for the greatest escape ever!

COMPETITION No.2

WIN 1,002 AIR MILES AWARDS PLUS

A SPECIAL EDITION OF THE NEXT EPISODE, *Coffey's Hands*, SIGNED BY STEPHEN KING

Call 0881 88 77 66

with your answers to the following questions and you could escape to a destination of your choice.

Which of the following events will happen in the next episode...

1. Percy Wetmore cruelly reaps his revenge on Delacroix.

2. William Wharton is the best-behaved prisoner on *The Green Mile*.

3. Paul Edgecombe becomes terminally ill with a urinary infection.

Tie-Breaker:

In 20 words or less, describe the continuing plot of *The Green Mile*...

Telephone lines close MIDNIGHT 23 May 1996

*The serial thriller
continues next month . . .*

STEPHEN KING'S
THE GREEN MILE:
Part Three
Coffey's Hands

Welcome back to E Block, the deadliest place this side of the electric chair, where assaults are a daily grind and miracles are soon to happen. Paul Edgecombe has become increasingly curious about John Coffey, the brutal killer of two girls. But Coffey reveals something extraordinary, and life on the Green Mile may never be the same again.

To Be Continued . . .

Visit *The Green Mile* on the Internet!
http://www.greenmile.com